For my Rainbow Baby, Jember Dove Shiferaw,

and to all of the Rainbow Babies of the world.

Daydreamers
PRESS

www.daydreamerspress.com

Manufactured in the United States of America

ISBN: 978-0-9996613-0-7

Dream a RAINBOW

By Carlotta Penn

Illustrated by Joelle Avelino

Rainbow, blue skies

Open up your sleepy eyes

In the clouds, a miracle

A promise for you and me

Red, orange, yellow, green

So much beauty I can see

Shines through you

Shines for you

A RAINBOW

Slide down, feel the sun

You are the gift of my dreams!

Rainbow, blue skies

Open up your sleepy eyes.

In the clouds, a miracle

A promise for you and me

Blue, indigo, violet

As magical as life can get

Colors of you

Colors for you

A **rainbow!** Slide down, feel the sun
Live the life of your dreams!

Rainbow, blue skies

Open up your sleepy eyes

In the clouds, a miracle

A promise for you and me

Bird, bumblebee, butterfly

Happy and free, way up high

Flying to you...

You can fly, too...

My Rainbow

Climb up, touch the sky...

Tell me,
what is your **dream?**

This book was inspired in part by my experience as the mother of a Rainbow Baby-- a child born after miscarriage. Thousands of women and their partners suffer pregnancy and infant loss every day, and it is a heartbreaking experience. The rainbow metaphor represents a dream come true, a promise delivered. I sang the words of this story to baby Jember throughout my pregnancy and was blessed to welcome her into the world on September 9th, 2016. My dream is for Jember to live a life filled with love, adventure, personal enrichment, and service to others. Daydreaming is my beloved pastime.

Carlotta Penn, PhD

@daydreamerspress

Made in the USA
Lexington, KY
07 December 2017